For Hannah, the original snow angel
—FCS

For Adelaide and Delia
—TB

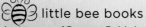 little bee books

An imprint of Bonnier Publishing USA
251 Park Avenue South, New York, NY 10010
Text copyright © 2017 by Fran Cannon Slayton
Illustrations copyright © 2017 by Tracy Bishop
LITTLE BEE BOOKS is a trademark of Bonnier Publishing USA, and associated
colophon is a trademark of Bonnier Publishing USA.
Manufactured in China LEO 0817
First Edition
10 9 8 7 6 5 4 3 2 1

Library of Congress Cataloging-in-Publication Data
Names: Slayton, Fran Cannon, author. | Bishop, Tracy, illustrator.
Title: Snowball moon / by Fran Cannon Slayton; illustrated by Tracy Bishop.
Description: First edition. | New York, NY: Little Bee Books, [2017]
Summary: When the lights go out one snowy night, neighborhood friends get
together for sledding, building forts, and more under the bright full moon.
Identifiers: LCCN 2016047314 | Subjects: | CYAC: Stories in rhyme. |
Snow—Fiction. | Family life—Fiction. | Moon—Fiction.
BISAC: JUVENILE FICTION / Concepts / Seasons. | JUVENILE FICTION /
Holidays & Celebrations / Christmas & Advent. | JUVENILE FICTION / Family /
General (see also headings under Social Issues).
Classification: LCC PZ8.3.S63188 Sno 2017 | DDC [E]—dc23
LC record available at https://lccn.loc.gov/2016047314

ISBN 978-1-4998-0495-9

littlebeebooks.com
bonnierpublishingusa.com

Snowball Moon

BY FRAN CANNON SLAYTON

ILLUSTRATED BY TRACY BISHOP

little bee books

Snowy night . . .
firelight.

Cozy flames,
friendly games.

Lights go out –
a scream! A shout!

Every eye
on the sky.

Snowball moon,
bright as noon.

Mittens, boots,
warm snowsuits.

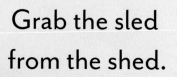

Grab the sled
from the shed.

Race outside
for a ride.

Down the hill,
winter thrill.

Frozen lake –
where's the brake?

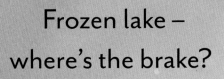

Slide and slip . . .
double flip!

Upside down,
spinning 'round.

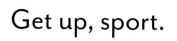

Get up, sport.

Build a fort.

Snowball fight.
What a night!

Frosty fun,
nearly done.

One more ride . . .

warm inside.

Rosy nose,
icy toes.

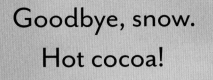

Goodbye, snow.
Hot cocoa!

Droopy eyes,
snowflake skies.

Counting sheep . . .
fall asleep.

Sleepyheads,
dreams of sleds.

Come back soon,
snowball moon!

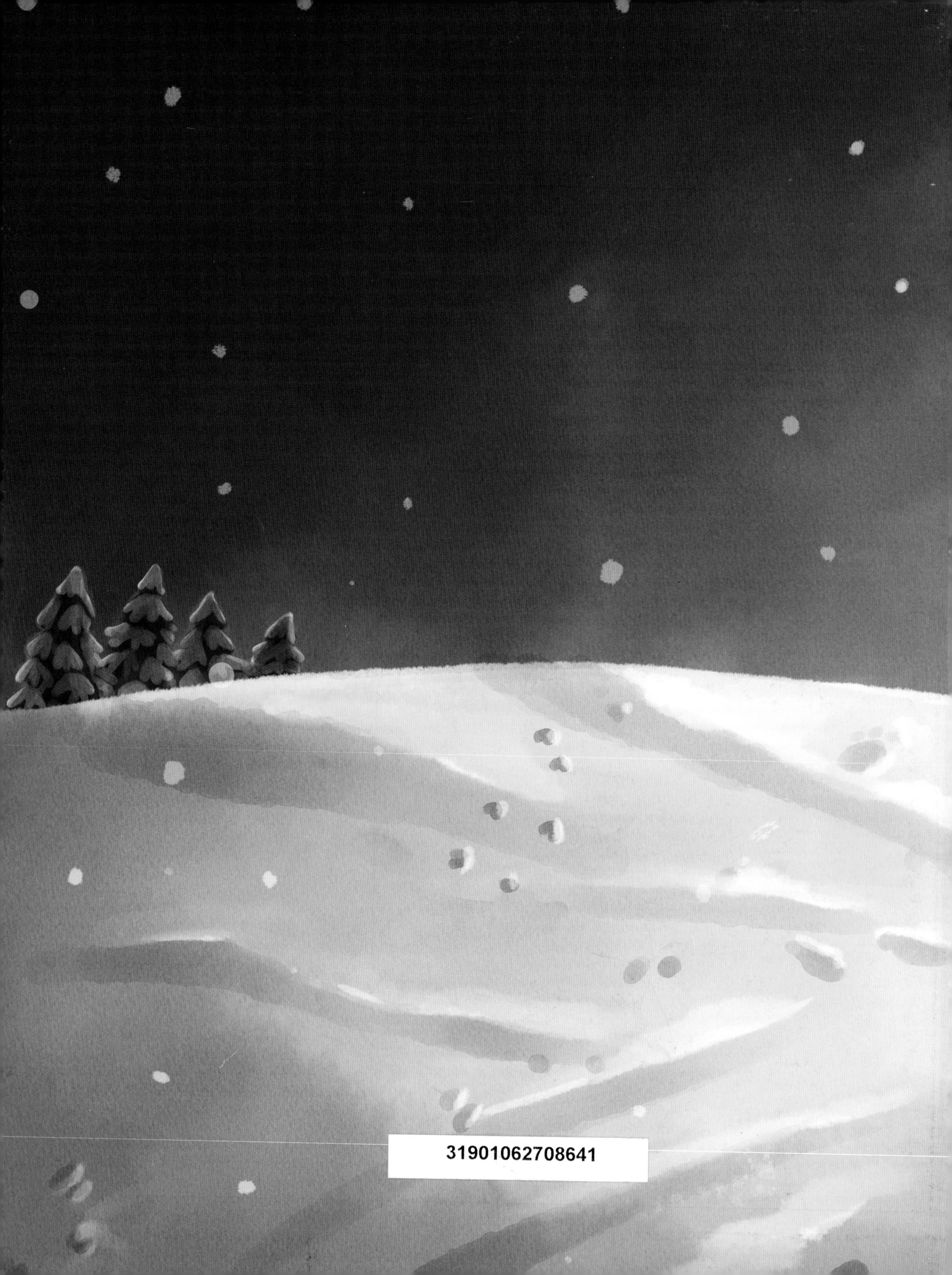